Dear Parents,

Welcome to the Scholastic Reader series. We have taken over 80 years of experience with teachers, parents, and children and put it into a program that is designed to match your child's interests and skills.

Level 1—Short sentences and stories made up of words kids can sound out using their phonics skills and words that are important to remember.

Level 2—Longer sentences and stories with words kids need to know and new "big" words that they will want to know.

Level 3—From sentences to paragraphs to longer stories, these books have large "chunks" of texts and are made up of a rich vocabulary.

Level 4—First chapter books with more words and fewer pictures.

It is important that children learn to read well enough to succeed in school and beyond. Here are ideas for reading this book with your child:

- Look at the book together. Encourage your child to read the title and make a prediction about the story.
- Read the book together. Encourage your child to sound out words when appropriate. When your child struggles, you can help by providing the word.
- Encourage your child to retell the story. This is a great way to check for comprehension.
- Have your child take the fluency test on the last page to check progress.

Scholastic Readers are designed to support your child's efforts to learn how to read at every age and every stage. Enjoy helping your child learn to read and love to read.

—**Francie Alexander**
Chief Education Officer
Scholastic Education

For Barbara, of course,
with a hug for Emilie.
— S.B.

Text copyright © 1992 by Sheri Brownrigg.
Illustrations copyright © 1992 by Meredith Johnson.
Activities copyright © 2003 Scholastic Inc.

All rights reserved. Published by Scholastic Inc.
SCHOLASTIC, CARTWHEEL BOOKS, and associated logos are trademarks
and/or registered trademarks of Scholastic Inc.

Library of Congress Cataloging-in-Publication Data is available.

ISBN 0-590-43904-9

20 19 18 17 16 15 14 13   07
Printed in the U.S.A.   23
First printing, April 1992

All Tutus Should Be Pink

by Sheri Brownrigg
Illustrated by Meredith Johnson

Scholastic Reader — Level 2

SCHOLASTIC INC.
New York   Toronto   London   Auckland   Sydney
Mexico City   New Delhi   Hong Kong   Buenos Aires

I love my new tutu!

It's pink.

I had another pink tutu,
but it got too small for me.

My dog Pepe-Pierre
wears it now.

Emily has a pink tutu, too.

She's the best friend
I ever had.

We wear our tutus everywhere.

To the grocery store.

To the movies.

Even to the beach.

The real reason
we have our tutus
is dance class.

Our favorite person is
our dance teacher,
Ms. Yvonne.

She used to be a famous
pink tutu dancer.

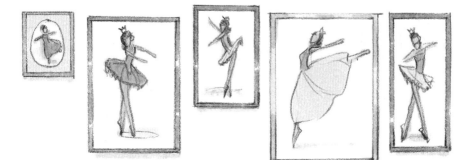

We know this because
there are pictures of her
at the studio.

We want to grow up to be
famous pink tutu dancers, too.

But I think we
would wear our tutus
even if we were
truck drivers!

Dance class looks like fun,
but it is hard.

Sometimes it's so hard,
Emily thinks she might faint.
And we want to quit.

Then we look at ourselves
in the mirror and see how
great we look.

And we keep on dancing.

Tutus make a magic *swoosh* sound
every time we move.

Sometimes we move a little extra
to make extra *swooshes*.

Others in class
wear their tutus
only on stage.

For Emily and me,
all the world is a stage.

After dance class
we are so famished!

We need to eat ice cream.
Strawberry only, please!

If we drop some on our tutus,
it doesn't matter.

They're pink, too.

That's why
all tutus should be pink.
I love my new tutu!